The Flyaway Blanket

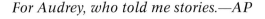

For Audrey, who told me stories.—AP

For my family and friends, who keep me drawing.—EP

Published by
MAGINATION PRESS
An Educational Publishing Foundation Book
American Psychological Association
750 First Street, NE
Washington, DC 20002
For more information about our books, including a complete catalog,
please write to us, call 1-800-374-2721,
or visit our website at www.apa.com/pubs/magination.

Book design by Susan K. White
Printed by Worzalla, Stevens Point, WI

Library of Congress Cataloging-in-Publication Data
Peterkin, Allan.
The flyaway blanket / by Allan Peterkin ; illustrated by Emmeline Pidgen.
p. cm.
ISBN-13: 978-1-4338-1047-3 (hardcover)
ISBN-10: 1-4338-1047-6 (hardcover)
ISBN-13: 978-1-4338-1046-6 (pbk.)
ISBN-10: 1-4338-1046-8 (pbk.)
1. Attachment behavior in children. 2. Security (Psychology) in children.
3. Mother and child. I. Pidgen, Emmeline. II. Title.
BF723.A75.P48 2012
155.9'24--dc22   2011011079
Manufactured in the United States of America
10 9 8 7 6 5 4 3 2 1

The Flyaway Blanket

by Allan Peterkin, MD

illustrated by Emmeline Pidgen

MAGINATION PRESS • WASHINGTON, DC

American Psychological Association

It was a beautiful morning with just a little breeze, so Jake and his mother decided to hang the laundry outside to dry.

Momma sang softly as
she pinned socks and towels
and t-shirts to the line:

time to fly, touch the sky, fly up,

high up, wave goodbye

Momma helped Jake hang his special blanket.

At first, Jake didn't want to let go.

The blanket was extra soft
from so much love,
and from Momma's gentle washings.

Momma told Jake the blanket would be dry in no time.

She asked him to come sit in the sun with her.

As Momma sang,
they both got sleepy.

time to fly,
touch the sky

No sooner had Jake
closed his eyes, than

whoosh!

Jake's blanket got snatched by the wind.

It flew high up into the sky.

First it brushed against the apple tree, where a mother bird was feeding her babies.

Apple blossoms dropped onto their heads like little hats.

They all watched as the blanket
sailed higher.

It flew into the meadow,
where a calf was shivering by the stream.

His momma snuggled close, trying to warm him up.

But *whoosh!* The wind caught it again!

The calf watched it fly into the farmer's garden.

Moo!
Moo!
Moo!

A mother rabbit and her baby
were chomping on a big turnip.

The blanket tickled their big ears
but did not stay.

So the bunnies jumped higher than ever, trying to catch it.

The blanket flew on, and landed in a flower patch.

A puppy grabbed the blanket and took it over to his momma.

They played tug of war.

When both let go for just one second,

whoosh!

The blanket leapt into the sky.

Woof! Woof! Woof!

The wind changed direction and
the blanket flew past the puppy,

Past the bunny,

Past the calf,

And their mommas.

They all followed:

time to fly, touch the sky, fly up, high up

The baby birds saw the
blanket coming back.

Chirp! Chirp! Chirp!

Jake was still asleep.

Wake up! Wake up!

What if Jake's special
blanket flew away and

waved goodbye

forever?

Suddenly, the momma bird flew straight up into the bright sky.

She circled the blanket as all the others looked on.

Then she gave it a little tug.

Down down down down tumbled the flyaway blanket...

right to where
it belonged.

Note to Parents

At its heart, *The Flyaway Blanket* is a simple story about the strength of the bonds between parents and their children. Often, children have a favorite blanket or soft toy they cuddle at night and carry with them everywhere. These transitional or comfort objects have been shown to play an important role in helping children to explore the world and become more independent as they grow toward adolescence. Transitional objects symbolize a parent's love and become a familiar presence that allows children to soothe themselves in new situations or when they feel alone or insecure. Every well-worn blanket becomes a treasure that is irreplaceable, and each has a unique story composed over time by the boy or girl who loves it.

In this charmingly illustrated story, a child's favorite blanket is picked up by the wind and carried away. The blanket flies through the neighborhood and passes many different animal mothers and babies, eventually returning to its original owner to be cherished and loved.

About the Author

Allan Peterkin, MD, is a Toronto-based physician and writer. He is Associate Professor of Psychiatry and Family Medicine and Head of the Health, Arts, and Humanities at the University of Toronto. Dr. Peterkin is the author of several children's books, including, *What About Me? When Brothers and Sisters Get Sick*, also published by Magination Press.

About the Illustrator

Emmeline Pidgen graduated in 2010 from University College Falmouth, and is now making her way through the jungle of the freelance world, trading snippets of her imagination so she can buy cereal, floral teacups, and dinosaur toys.

About Magination Press

Magination Press publishes self-help books for kids and the adults in their lives. Magination Press is an imprint of the American Psychological Association, the largest scientific and professional organization representing psychologists in the United States and the largest association of psychologists worldwide.